T0123331

MEXICAN DRUG SCANDAL

Marjorie May Pearson

authorHOUSE®

AuthorHouse™
1663 Liberty Drive
Bloomington, IN 47403
www.authorhouse.com
Phone: 833-262-8899

Published by AuthorHouse 07/12/2021

ISBN: 978-1-6655-3061-3 (sc)
ISBN: 978-1-6655-3062-0 (hc)
ISBN: 978-1-6655-3066-8 (e)

Library of Congress Control Number: 2021913250

How much longer?" Marcus flicked his cigarette onto the parking lot pavement and ground the smoke out with the toe of his tennis shoe.

"Five maybe eight minutes," Kyle said taking another stick of gum out of his pack to add to the piece he had been chewing for the last twenty minutes.

"Are you sure these guys can be trusted?" Marcus leaned against the brick wall in the alley where they had been standing, pacing, talking since they got a call from Ian Mendez about the drug shipment.

Kyle offered a spearmint gum stick behind his back "Ian trusts them."

Marcus grabbed the stick, "Yeah. Well I'm tired of waiting."

He took the gum from the foil wrapper, balling the wrapper and folding the soft stick onto his tongue and begun enjoying the flavor. To chew was something to be done. Marcus thumped the foil ball down to the pavement across to the other brick-building wall.

"Me too," Kyle agreed. He had been running these trips with Marcus for four months. It still felt new, but he loved the adrenaline rush doing these adventures gave him. The girls he could afford at the casinos were worth the cash he received too.

Las Vegas was truly the sin city. Gangsters trailed cops, not the other way around like in Chicago. Kyle hated working in Chicago. Only best part about the windy city was a girl named Valerie. Well a tomboy-girl. She wore about as much clothes as the casino ladies did but her black leather showed something more pleasing to him.

Kyle had a crush on Valerie ever since their group met in March. He wondered if she was doing a job now or if possibly she would be coming to California for this job. Or Nevada... Kyle hoped they met in California...less cops.

They might be trailed less by cops here, but Kyle liked to look on the most positive side. Once they crossed into California, the L.V.P.D. jurisdiction was long gone anyway. They could swap vehicles and not even be suspected by the telephoned cops in California.

Kyle looked down at his watch again. Nine thirty-four. It was balmy and the gum was starting to lose the strong spearmint flavor.

"How much longer?" Marcus asked again.

"Any minute now."

"It's time?"

"Yeah. Its Nine-thirty-five just....." Kyle watched the digits change, staring at his watch again. "Now."

"Good grief. You ladies still here?" Mandi, Ian's younger brother's girlfriend trotted between the brick walls holding a camouflaged purse under one arm next to her frilly dark green belly showing tee shirt.

"Where's Ian?" Marcus walked up behind Kyle, arms crossed, gum held to one side of his mouth, resting between his jaw and his row of teeth.

"Wherever he wants to be," Mandi sassed, flipping her hair back and pulling a compact mirror from her short-jean shorts pocket like it was a caliber in a street fight. She powdered her nose and looked relatively calm.

"Come on, Mand, where's the gang? Where's the junk?" Asked Kyle as he stood against the street light pole, pulling the gum from his mouth and tossing it at a garbage dumpster, not taking his eyes off of cosmetic girl before him. Randy would kill them if they even thought sexual things to do to his girl.

"Randy will be here shortly. Ya'll chill a min." She closed her compact mirror and tucked it back in her side

4

shorts pocket. "What time you got?" She asked, nodding at Kyle.

"Nine-thirty-six."

"I hate it when he plays games," Marcus hooked his thumbs on the side of his black leather pants and looked from one end of the alley to the other. One was a wooden fence and over that fence was a deli, where Kyle had hid out so many times he lost count.

On the other side of the alley was Broad Street - Vegas' link to all the casino roads. The building where Marcus has been leaning earlier was the back of an apartment building.

The other building that Mandi was closest to was a grocery store. Behind Mandi was a gray metal door that was locked. Kyle checked it when they decided to stand here. Their usual meeting place for the gang. He could have used a better snack then spearmint gum like he always kept with him.

"Patience, my main man," Mandi mocked Randy's usual comment to Marcus. She winked and Marcus kicked a rock down towards the wooden fence.

"I hate waiting," Marcus mumbled repeating his annoyance again.

"Then don't wait anymore. Go home," Mandi teased.

"I ain't doin' that." Marcus growled looking up at Mandi's smirk.

Fewer men meant a better pay split.

"Patience Man," Kyle said calming his friend. "Ian's never steered us wrong before."

"I know it."

"Then shut up. You're getting on my nerves," Mandi said flatly. She rubbed her hand over her belly button as if it made her style better somehow. Kyle tried not to notice. Marcus stepped towards her and Mandi backed herself to the grocery store brick wall.

"If he's any later...." Marcus started closing in on Mandi. Kyle stepped away from the pole he leaned on and grabbed Marcus' shirttail, pulling him back, and then taking hold of his shoulder.

"We'll wait until he gets here. His girl won't stay any longer than she's needed." Kyle looked hard into Marcus' eyes.

"She'll stay just as long as she's needed," a snap from the fence end of the alley had Marcus turning quickly pulling his pocket blade out and turning the silver towards the man coming from them. Marcus relaxed, pocketing his blade, and Kyle leaned again on the pole as Ian and Randy walked into the beam of light, followed by Martin, Kat, Tony, and Shawn (the only black person in their gang).

Katerina Mavromatis was a friend of May, Tony's girl. She was working the late shift at the pizza place inside the Bellagio where the supplies were coming from. Coke was going to be shipped in ten pizza boxes, May was supposed to be getting.

Kat wore slim jeans with a chain belt and a waist length short-sleeved blue shirt with a white collar wore high on the back of her neck. Her hair was braided in a single ponytail down her neck and to the middle of her back.

Mandi eyed her then smiled at her man, Randy and his brother Ian. "Baby."

"You behaving, Chick?" Tony walked over to the wall, keeping outside the beam of the dim streetlight. He patted Mandi's side, Kyle knew he was looking for that pack of cigs she had let Marcus have earlier that morning.

"I gave them to Marc, stop it," Mandi pushed Tony away by this shoulder.

"Marcus!" Tony acting like he was dunking a basketball. Marcus pulled the cig pack out of his black tee shirt chest pocket and tossed it into Tony's hands.

"Heaven is cigs," Tony took two cigs out of the pack, putting one behind his ear for later and one in his mouth for present time, he looked at Marcus then Mandi, as if he couldn't decide where to get a light.

"Tone you don't carry nothin on you do you?" Kat asked smartly walking towards him, pulling a lighter from her back jeans pocket and opening a flame for Tony.

"Thanks Babe." Tony said through clenched teeth as he lit the end and puffed smoke down through his nostrils.

Kat flipped the lighter back into her jeans back pocket. "Notta prob."

"How's it goin' Babe?" Randy walked over and tugged Mandi under his arm, as he hung one hand down in front of her neck, leaning on the brick wall with her. Marcus crossed his arms and looked at Ian. "So?"

Ian looked around at the eight of them.

"May's getting the boxes." Tony nodded as Ian turned his gaze around at them all. "Tony will help her at the end of her shift. Kat will be bringing Liz and Val," Kyle's ears twitched but he didn't move from off the post. He started chewing his gum nervously at the sound of his favorite girl's name. Valerie was in on this. Elizabeth was coming from New Orleans and Valerie from Chicago. Kyle didn't know where the cocaine was coming from yet, but he did know how it was getting to Mexico. Kevin would be up to join Kyle on his way by morning. They had a lil less than twelve hours to get the coke pizza boxes in Kevin's truck. Where was Kevin? Kyle stopped his thoughts and looked at Ian as he explained the rest.

"Shawn and Martin are going to meet Kevin at the state line at 1 A M." Martin nodded at Ian. Shawn crossed his arms looking around at Mandi and Randy whispering to each other. Mandi would smile but no giggles were heard so that Ian was heard. Shawn turned his gaze upon Ian again.

"Marcus will come with me, Randy, and Mand. Does anyone not understand anything I've said?"

Randy spoke up with his arm still around his girl's neck, his hand hovering just over her cleavage, "Tell them about the cut, Boss."

Ian smiled. "Oh yeah."

"Yeah, Bro!" Tony said excitedly. "Tell us about our cut in the bank roll."

"Kevin will be receiving the hundred grand at Mexico. You will each get an envelope with – yes – cash, greenbacks; you name it, in them. Depending on the trouble we have, which shouldn't be any. This should be a clean, smooth trip. The envelopes will be given out one at a time. One every day will be picked up at this alley. If two of you show up at the same time, I don't care if you are a couple," Ian eyed Tony then Randy. "I don't care if you were best friends in college," he eyed Kyle. Kyle stared back determined not to break eye contact. "Only one envelope will go out a day. I won't have but one on me. I'll give you one. If you want to talk some afterwards fine. Or you can just leave. After the job you are free to go home, get a job, buy a house… I don't care. The job will be over and done with. Any other questions?"

"Can anybody quit?" Her voice was a surprise. Kyle stared at Mandi. He could tell everyone else was too.

"Yeah. You thinkin' about quittin' on us, Mandi?" Ian said slowly, but then looked at his brother. Randy shrugged and looked back at Mandi.

"Naw, I was just wondering. Marcus was acting like he wanted to quit." Kyle chuckled silently against his post.

"I was not!" Marcus growled.

"Were you?" Ian looked at Marcus, staring him down. Marcus knew not to move. He looked over at Kyle.

"No, Ian. Marcus just thought ya'll were late is all."

"Gee thanks, friend."

"Maybe ya'll were early," Ian smiled looking at Shawn. Shawn nodded smiling back at Marcus.

"Ya'll were just early," Shawn agreed.

"Maybe my watch is a little slow," Kyle told Marcus.

"Maybe you should fix it," Marcus growled, annoyed that he was center of attention for everyone's jokes.

Kyle didn't say anything in return. He knew that Marcus was just under a lot of heat like he was in every job.

"So everyone's in?" Randy looked at his girl then everyone else. Kyle nodded and everyone else did too.

"I do have one question," Kat spoke up, not surprising Kyle. He would have thought she would have a question at first when Ian asked everyone.

"Shoot," Ian said smiling curiously at her.

"What should we wear for Mexico temps? Same thing we wear here?"

Kyle smiled. He thought Kat knew that she wasn't invited. He might invite Valerie, but he doubted she'd be interested. He doubted Ian would be interested.

"Girls aren't going to Mexico. Are they Kyle?" Ian asked, noting Kyle's grin.

"Nope," Kyle looked at Kat. "Two guys are going to Mexico and two guys are coming back. No girls are allowed on the truck." He winked at Kat. "No room anyway."

"I'm sure I could find a spot," Mandi said loud enough for everyone to hear but Kyle could tell by looking at her staring in Randy's direction it had only been for her man.

Some chuckles floated around the group then it got quiet again.

"Randy go start the coupe. See if Mandi wants a ride over to Tony's."

"Do ya Babe?"

"I can't. I'm working, 'member?" Mandi leaned over and kissed Randy's lips regretfully.

"We can drive ya over there," Randy suggested.

"Man, she works the other direction," Ian contested.

"Yeah two miles," Randy argued.

"Yeah… See you at the site later, Mand."

Mandi grinned, seeming not to care about Ian's words. "It's alright Randy. I still love you for trying." She kissed her man again, and arms wrapped around bodies this time. Kyle took his eyes off of them as he heard Marcus growl.

"I don't want to ride with him," Marcus whispered low to only Kyle's hearing as everyone started to leave or talk about leaving. Shawn was asking Martin where he was getting a taxi. Kyle directed his attention back to his colleague.

"Man, it's a job. You gotta make these little sacrifices you don't like sometimes. You could always ask to go with Shawn and…"

"I ain't riding with a nigger."

"Shut up, man. You know very well Shawn ain't like them street blacks in Guadalupe."

"I'm already tired and don't want to deal with anything that comes out of Martin's or his mouth." Marcus countered his behavior. He was cranky because he hadn't gone to bed last night. He had played with a chick until nine this morning, then spent the day with Kyle. If he hadn't driven here he could have taken a road nap from their hotel.

"Just go with them, Marc. I'll see ya later. Okay?"

"Marc you coming with us. Come on," Ian called. Kyle looked around and noticed it was just he and Ian and Tony. Tony stood by the grocery store metal side door as if going to try to open it. He pulled something out of his pocket and Kyle smiled. He had a pick kit.

"See ya," Marcus replied to Kyle.

"Yeah, okay." Kyle said half listening to his partner's whining goodbyes. He walked over to Tony as Marcus and Ian left. Mandi had gone. Kyle wasn't sure which way. He hadn't noticed her leave.

"That a stainless steel?" He asked walking up behind Tony.

"Yeah. You got one?"

"Naw," Kyle watched the metal door swing open with Mandi on the other side. "Mind if I join ya'll?"

"Okay but Mandi's never had a threesome..." Tony winked.

"And never will. Hurry up, Tony and put your cig out. They got sprinklers in here." Mandi walked back into the dark back room of the closed grocery. It had closed at seven like all the other family owned shops in Vegas. They might just get one night in jail... if they get caught. If they did get caught the plan was always ask stupid questions to the cops and act drunk. Don't ever run if there's a cop around. Mandi would hang on one of them like she couldn't walk. Like they were lovers. When Randy heard about those times Tony was the one who got hanged on when Mandi was supposed to be at work, and really had told him that because she hated riding with Ian – the boss – the serious guy in the group, Randy was pissed. And the guy she hung on, usually Tony, got the same old lecture about Mandi's job in the group. She's a decoy and not to be toyed with. Tony didn't ever act like he cared what Randy said. But he always told Randy to calm down, that he understood.

"I might like you all wet wearing all that leather and pleather," Tony shot back as her body disappeared behind stock boxes.

"Shush," Mandi whispered running her fingers over the boxes, squinting at the names. Kyle closed the door until only a crack was left. Tony had zipped his pick kit and tucked it back in his hooded shirt for later, to lock up.

"Any idea where the boss and brother is going with my colleague, Tony?"

"Back to the big house would be my guess. Ian doesn't like to dawdle around doing nothing or play games like we are doing."

"Great." Kyle showed his bothered attitude.

"Problem with that?"

"Marcus tried to get out of the ride." Kyle looked as Tony picked up a vase full of flowers then set it back down. The flowers looked wilted and he shook his head as if deciding not on a decision.

"They wanted Marc with them. He has some explaining to do before he can be trusted at the site."

Kyle put down a pineapple Mandi had passed up. "What explaining?"

"His time in jail back in ninety-eight." Tony looked at peaches and plums in a basket beside the cashier register.

"That was for nothing, really," Kyle sighed thinking it was bigger than that.

"Is that what he told you or what you know?" Tony walked back into the back room of the grocery store as a car passed the front glass, headlights at full blast, enough to show shadows where they shouldn't be.

"That's what I know, cause he told me," Kyle said determined not to be frazzled by Tony's accusation.

"You never check backgrounds when Marcus tells you what he deems the honest truth, do you man?"

Mandi looked up at them as if just following their lead. Kyle looked her face over trying to see if she was in on this accusation too. She held up both hands and turned toward the bread department of boxes.

"No." Kyle answered Tony's question in all seriousness. Their fun was losing its touch tonight.

"What time you got?" Tony pointed at Kyle keeping up with his job time. He had to meet May in forty-two minutes.

"Ten eighteen. What did Ian find in a background check on Marcus?" Kyle changed the subject back to his friend's case. He felt sorry for what Marcus was going through now. The questions, the shouting; Marcus would probably have a black eye, if Ian or Randy didn't later tonight.

"Randy was checking our backgrounds. Ian doesn't do computer work. He thinks up ideas. He knows the sources. He never looked up backgrounds before but this time he started thinking he better, so he did. I've served six months before for smoking coke. May knows about it. She was mad. Ian was mad. I don't do it anymore. He's already talked to me about if he could handle packaging coke without double-crossing him. He put May on the job as assistant to me, not just because she can supply boxes from her job and we are dating, but because he knows if I sneak anything she'll see it. He's just giving Marcus the one, two, three about double-crossing and the punishments that go with it."

"What was found in Marcus' background?" Kyle repeated.

Mandi walked over with three loaves of French bread. "Any croissants?" Tony asked looking over and taking the long bread loaves from her.

"Nope," Mandi replied standing there.

"Go look out."

"I know what ya'll are discussing."

"I know you do, go see if there is a cop patrolling out front." Tony said nodding his head towards the front room of the store.

"Fine." Mandi trotted off angry to the front of the store. "Nope."

"Just stay there." Tony said looking back at Kyle. "Marcus ever tell you about a wreck he had in Phoenix two years ago."

"Yeah. Drunk driver hit a guy full force. Happened while I was moving my things from Brazil to Phoenix. Marcus was coming to meet me and passed by that wreck. Drunk driver ran and later they found out there was a girl involved in the front seat of the other car. She died but her boyfriend lived to report the accident. Said he didn't see the driver. Marcus said it was a bad wreck. Engine's totaled on both cars. So?" Kyle folded his arms.

"Marcus ever tell you 'bout the cars involved in that wreck?"

"No. I didn't care at the time. It was an interesting story. I didn't even get a paper. Marcus got one. Threw it away after two months I think. Wanted me to read it. I never did because I never got around to it. Nothin to worry about Tony, what's up?"

"Kyle come on outside with me." Tony took the three loaves of bread to the cracked side door. Kyle didn't want to put pieces together right now. What Tony was saying wasn't making sense and right now that's how Kyle liked it. He followed Tony out the door. "See you in ten minutes, Mandi."

"Right," Mandi sounded mad still but on the job. She was going out the front window. The same way she had been in, Kyle betted. She was so small it was like a cat through a two inch cracked door.

Tony shut the door and locked it back from the inside the checked to make sure it was going to hold. It did. "Marcus was the drunk driver that ran." Tony turned back around. Kyle turned towards the beam of streetlight coming down on the alley.

"No. You're wrong. Marcus doesn't run from his..." But Kyle couldn't finish his sentence. Marcus had run from problems before. He blew a job in Arizona, that's why they were in Nevada now. That's how they had met Tony and Ian and Randy. Kyle swore.

"I'm sorry man. I know trust runs deep with you."

"He know now?" Mandi came around the corner with a single rose.

"Yeah," Tony's sour answer was because it hadn't been ten minutes yet. But he looked at the rose. "That for me?"

"For your girl. I saw you pick up that wilted vase in there." Mandi handed Tony the rose and he handed her two loaves of French bread. She approached Kyle cautiously. "Hungry?"

Kyle grabbed his loaf. "Thanks." He still couldn't believe Marcus was wanted in Arizona for killing a girl and injuring a boy. He'd be on the inside with Ian now, like an idealist. He wouldn't have a choice. He couldn't leave the group until Kyle came back from Mexico. Kyle planned not to mess around with coming back. Not to take his time. He had to come back for his friend's sake. He started walking off towards the street.

"Let him go," he heard Tony tell Mandi.

"You sure are bossy tonight." Their voices were fading as he looked down at the street, making his way to his car that would take him to Ian's house. Marcus was still his friend. And Kyle felt sorry for Marcus.

J ust go with them, Man," Marcus' growl startled Kyle worse than the black eye he could see bruising his left eye. Marc held an ice pack to his eye as he had been doing before he started talking. Kyle winced and stood a few feet away from Marcus. Ready for a temper to fly. Ready for a friendship to end because of a job.

"You still on the job at least," Kyle said dragging his words along.

"Oh yeah! At half what you're getting! Guess what nigger is getting my other half?"

"Watch it, Boy," Randy said from the corner of Ian's pad. They were waiting here until Martin and Shawn returned from picking up Kevin. A rest stop and information center was there, Kevin would be there with his makeshift white pizza van, and they called the truck. Kevin wished it were a truck. May and him started calling it "the truck" and the name stuck. A little inside joke Kyle never cared to know the whole story.

Kyle looked up from scooting the toe of his shoe across Ian's tile living room floor. The floor looked recently mopped, or maybe this room was only used for gang meetings. "Sorry man. You can split mine. Even take half if you want," Kyle offered truthfully, thinking it was better to lose half of a lot of dough then a good friend he knew through his college years in Guadalupe.

"I don't want your cash man. And I don't want this black eye or that black nigger running my shifts," Marcus spat back at Randy's corner. He was gone though. Disappeared into the shadows like he was known to do.

Marc cussed and looked back at Kyle as if he had been betrayed and embarrassed by those he trusted most.

Kyle walked over to the sliding glass door that led out on the poolside porch. Ian was swimming laps to relax himself. Randy sat at a glass picnic table with an umbrella in the middle of the table. He was talking on a cell phone, Kyle wondered if he was talking to Mandi or the guys that were delivering the drugs later on tonight. Could be Martin or Shawn lost on the way to the state line. He would think Martin wouldn't get lost. Maybe in the dark, Kyle chuckled silently. He knew Marcus was behind him, could come up and hit him, but Kyle stood there, feet planted ready for a hit. He'd deserve it. Ian would have fought him in the alley. It would have looked like Kyle was protecting a brother for his crimes, even though at the time Kyle had no idea. He should be mad at Marcus for lying, but he wasn't. He was offered the paper by Marcus but seemed to not want to know. He was just busy, sadly, but truthfully. He wished he were the one with the black eye.

Randy closed his cell phone and Ian started up a ladder in the deep end of the pool. Randy handed his brother a cloth robe, Ian scooted into his flip-flops and Kyle moved back away from the door as they walked to the door. Kyle leaned against the fireplace brick chimney and looked around for Marcus. He heard a cluttering toward the kitchen and decided Marc had gone for more ice.

"Heard you looked up my bro's file," Kyle spoke as Randy led Ian into the living room. Ian stopped just as soon as Randy did, they turned toward Kyle at the same time and he prepared himself to repeat what he had said. He had interrupted their laughing.

"Marcus has no reason to be paid, yet we're paying him, Brazilian boy," Randy replied, his fists tightening on each side of his waist, the cell phone tucked in its clip on his belt.

"Mighty kind of you. Especially to give it to Shawn, the guy I'm guessing did your dirty work to his eye," Kyle nodded at Ian. Ian's eyebrow was raised in high curiosity.

His hands were still in his robe pockets and his legs were dripping on the tile floor same as when he had entered the house.

"Randy go finish your calls," Ian commanded. Randy looked back at his brother and received a nod.

"You heard him, California boy," Kyle mocked Randy's earlier comment. Kyle stood relaxed on the brick chimney.

Randy grimaced but followed his brother's orders and rounded the stair railing, taking two carpeted steps at a time up to the second floor where the bedrooms were.

"Dirty work, you call it, Kyle?" Ian sat down in a leather recliner, crossing his legs at his ankles, his hands still in his pockets. "Tony tell you what Marc was up to in Phoenix?"

"He caused a wreck and ran. So? He's my bro and you gave him a black eye for not being sober? For killing a girl?"

"He deserved what he got." Ian stated bluntly. "You want him to get paid still or you wish you had gotten his black eye?" Ian stared at Kyle.

"Both," Kyle stared back speaking just as bluntly.

"Did Randy tell you what Marcus calls Shawn? Did Shawn ever mess around with Marcus or does your bro have a special place in his mouth for black Americans?"

"He's been tripped up loads of times by them. He acts the way his Momma raised him. Just because he has bad manners ain't no reason to bruise his eye. Tony went to jail and he didn't get hit."

"He didn't cuss a member, either. He didn't smart his boss, and he didn't kill anyone."

"Naw, he was just taking the poison that killed his old man. He was dating May and threatening her life by making love to her. Naw, a member of the gang, Ian? He was just doing the dirty. You hit my bro. Either he gets all the money or we are both out."

Marcus came out of the kitchen," Whoa Kyle, what's up dude?"

"We're leaving."

"No you ain't," Ian stood up, the recliner wet from his dripping hair and wet robe. "He still want the whole seven thou plus. Fine. Don't be messing with our heads again though, boys. It isn't nice to keep the truth from your boss. You want a good lawyer if we get caught in the job right? I'll get you one, free of charge, but I gotta know you ain't dissing my members. You can't be hiding this junk, ya got it?"

Marcus nodded, "Yeah."

Kyle nodded. "Not a problem boss."

Randy came downstairs as Marcus reapplied another pack of ice to his eye and joined Kyle at the brick chimney wall. "Tony, May, and Mandi are headed to the site as we speak. Shawn called and said him and Martin and Kevin are half way to the site. Wanted to know if we needed them pick anyone else up. I told them we got it." Randy looked over at Kyle, staring curiously.

"Where's Kat right now?" Ian asked Randy to reacquire his attention, lifting it from Kyle's.

"McCarren, fixing to drive here and pick anyone who wants to ride backseat with three girls."

"They have the convertible right?"

"Yeah." Randy said slowly and Kyle caught on it right away.

"Give Kyle, Kat's number and have them meet you here, Kyle. You and Marcus don't mind riding with the three of them do you?"

"Not at all," Marcus replied in place of Kyle. Randy turned his gaze from Marcus to Kyle then gave out Kat's number and Kyle dialed it into his speed dial number four. He had yet to get any of them casino girls' numbers and his cell was just asking for a black book log. Maybe he could restock it with the gang girl's numbers. He walked into the game room, Marcus on his heels. Randy began arguing with his brother over the idea of the two colleagues riding with three gang girls.

"Kat? This is Kyle. Ian would like you to swing by here and pick up two hitchhikers."

"Oh really? Not sure we have the room for two hikers. Val's making room in the backseat for one guy and her though," Kat teased.

"Want to talk to Ian?" Kyle nagged.

"Not really. We'll let the hikers in the back. Let ya get to know our hairstyles better from that angle. Never rode backseat for me have ya, Kylee?"

Kyle hated that nickname, but if it got him to riding in a car with his girl Val, who he hadn't seen since last month's job, he didn't mind a little flying hair. "It will be fun, Kat, you know it."

He turned and looked at Marcus who was smiling though he held the ice pack to his eye. Kyle fingered the pool table chalk and then wiped the residue on the red felt tabletop. "See you in twenty minutes?" Kyle asked.

"Fifteen if the cops let us off for Val's flashing techniques," Kat hung up on that note. Kyle dared to call her back but didn't, on account on how his attention toward Valerie would look. He lowered the phone and hung up grinning back at his bro.

"They'll be here in twenty minutes."

"Five minutes late," Kyle teased Kat as he walked down the concrete path towards the curb where Ian's convertible sat. Val sat in between Martin's girlfriend, Elizabeth and Katerina, who drove the vehicle. She had a buttoned up tank tied around her belly button and faded blue jean shorts that looked the same brand as Liz's white long jeans: slim and fitting their legs, long and athletic. Even though Kyle couldn't see Liz's legs, he remembered her look like last month. This month's difference for Liz: she was wearing a smaller shirt and her hair was in a braid like Kat's hair. Val's hair mirrored the same braided style. No hair would be flying in Marc and his faces.

Marcus walked around the back of the convertible and Kat revved the engine of the little yellow cream-colored car. He jumped over the door and landed behind Liz in the back seat. Kyle copied his colleague's entrance and landed on the white leather seat behind Kat. "Cop decided to ask Valerie some questions," Katerina pulled out into the house street and then onto a highway that led to the interstate south of town. She yelled above the radio and wind, until Liz turned down the hard rock hits and she was just yelling over the wind. Kyle yelled back, "Not too bad I hope!"

"Naw! Liz got out and explained everything to him. Not a problem one bit! Was it Liz?" Kat gave a side-glance at Elizabeth. She smirked a smile that a federal judge wouldn't be able to distrust. They passed the mall over Boulevard and Kyle looked at the lights left on. Soon no lights would be on but the neon ones in main Vegas, and Kyle would be on his way to Mexico. He still wanted to ask Valerie to go with him, but now Marcus lay heavier on his mind, as a need to leave the states. Marcus could ride with them down to Guadalupe to stay with his Aunt; it was better than staying with the gang after Kyle was gone. He leaned over to ask Marcus this when Valerie spoke up, breaking all of Kyle's concentration.

"You look better without the go-tee!" He could see her smiling through the rearview mirror. That smile charmed him enough to reply.

"Thank ya, Ma'am." Kyle winked at her through the mirror. Kat had asked Liz something by leaning over in front of Val, while they had been returning grins through the mirror. Kyle could barely hear an answer through the wind. He looked at the road as Kat moved back into the far left lane. She wanted to drive as fast as possible. Eighty-five was legal, the eighty-nine he could see through her fingers wasn't.

"Katerina!" Kyle yelled as a warning.

"I know it, Kylee," Kat used that annoying nickname again. The only reason she got away with it and May didn't was because she dated him once; May had only flirted with him; while dating Tony. It had been a short flirtatious night and Kyle knew May only remembered stripping for him and having her clothes handed back to her. Nothing ever happened more than a little drunk fun. May only needed one round of gin to get her riled up. They had been celebrating Tony's first night out of jail and Tony had gone home at three A.M. kissing his girlfriend's forehead and waving at the gang. That had been three months ago. Kyle looked back up at Kat's speed-o-meter: Eighty-five was fine until they hit the highway. She'd need to slow down to seventy-five if they wanted to try to be on time if not a few minutes early. Another cop stop and one look at Marcus' eye and they would be at most, twenty minutes late. Kyle didn't need anymore trouble from Ian than he had. He sure as anything didn't need Randy thinking him and Valerie were smooching on the way here. He had a feeling Randy already thought that.

"Where'd Marc pick up the shiner?" Katerina yelled over the wind again, slowing down a bit to slide over three lanes into the exit ramp to take highway ninety-five south. "He didn't have that last night after I left Ian's pad!"

"Shawn," Marcus yelled as they pulled onto highway ninety-five.

"Want me to talk to him for ya," Liz offered turning her head inside the middle towards Valerie's ear.

"Would you?" Marcus flirted, grinning.

"I would if I knew the problem," Liz said at normal tone as Kat pulled into a gas station.

"You're kidding," Kyle said pulling himself up on top of the back seat. "You didn't get gas at the airport?" Kat had gotten out and was using Ian's ATM card on the pump. She grabbed the nozzle and stuck it in the car, then gazed up at Kyle with her 'you asked, I'll tell ya' look.

"Didn't need any then." She looked back down.

Kyle looked up at the fuel gauge. Fourth a tank. They would have died half way down the highway. He slid back down the backseat, wanting to grumble about females and how thinking never cooperated with them. But he kept his mouth shut. He cursed and looked at Marcus, who rolled his eyes. "Women," Marcus grumbled.

"We make mistakes just like you do," Liz argued. Valerie had scooted out of the seat and ran in the store. To use the bathroom, Kyle figured. He was wrong and bit his tongue for thinking women were all trouble. His woman was bringing back snacks. Only she threw the bag at Liz.

"They said we are the cause for being so slow," Liz told Valerie as she got back into the middle. Kat followed Val and buckled herself into the seat, cranking the convertible and resetting the mileage dial.

"Come on, Lizzy, I was jokin'," Marcus pleaded as hungry as Kyle was feeling.

"All that's in there is moon pies and soda pop," Valerie shouted in the back seat above the wind.

"Works for me," Kyle yelled, hoping his charm would get a pie and at least one soda for Marc and him both.

Liz threw the bag into the backseat right into Marc's lap. He took out a Dr. Pepper, two moon pies, and a Diet

Sprite. Marc looked at the Diet Sprite non-convincingly and handed it to Kyle to what seemed like apologetically. He mouthed a sorry and Kyle nodded back not wanting to end the moment him and Marcus were sharing. Kyle took one moon pie and the bag flew behind them. Kyle looked at it go, not hitting anyone considering there was no one to be hit behind them. They weren't even in a desert yet and the cars hadn't followed them. No one was going to Davis Dam this late at night. Or no one was taking the route Kat took. Valerie handed a not yet opened Barq's root beer to Kyle. He took it and she kept her hand back, waiting for her drink. "Sorry about the switch!" She yelled and looked to be smiling apologetic-like through the rearview mirror. Kyle winked at her and handed her diet Sprite he would have drank more pleasurably knowing it was Val's. She took the drink, shouted a thank you and all went quiet as eleven forty-five snack took over their mouths.

12:05 A.M. Kyle looked at his watch then out the window. They were still driving south on this empty highway. Marcus had fallen asleep in his corner, despite the cool wind blowing over them at seventy-five miles per hour. The girls were talking in the front seat and had turned on a hard rock station they knew Kyle would like, he guessed. He took to looking around more than listening. It was barely there anyway with the wind blowing past his ears. He was glad all the girls had braided their hair. Liz didn't have that much to braid and had two braided pigtails. He had noticed it when he got in the car, it just took to now to realize they had braided their hair for the windy ride.

Last time Kyle had seen dusty median and short grasses like this were in Mexico. He looked back up front, intending on making conversation with the girls if he had to yell over the wind. "Another twenty minutes you gals think?"

Valerie looked at him in the rearview mirror but the other girls didn't move. Katerina was leaning over, staring at the highway but her body language told Kyle she was listening to Liz. Liz was leaned over, without seatbelt, on Val's lap. Valerie turned her attention back to the front. Kyle scooted up on the edge of his seat. "What we discussing?"

Kat steered the convertible over the yellow line and for a few seconds Marcus talked in Spanish about not wanting to get up because his friends were big jerks. He placed his elbow under his head and seemed to be asleep again. Liz laughed, not only at Kat's driving but Marcus' announcement. Valerie looked in the mirror and since he was too close the back of their seats she looked sideways, at Kat but showing a smile for Kyle. Kat got them back in the right lane of the highway and tensed her shoulders. "Maybe I should have knocked first. Would you turn the radio off?"

Valerie complied and was smiling still. He loved that smile. "Maybe," she finally said when the radio wasn't booming.

"Try tapping our shoulder, Fur ball," Kat said tersely.

"Fur ball?" Kyle said feeling of his chin. He had grown a bit of a five o'clock shadow over the past few hours. He hadn't shaved earlier before the meeting. He was thinking about growing a go-tee or a thin mustache like Randy had. "Hmm." Kyle studied Kat's frown in the mirror. He leaned his head between her and Valerie's shoulder. Val didn't move but Kat started to roll her shoulder and Kyle could just see his nose bleeding at the site from Kat's sharp elbow into his nose. He leaned back and she missed. She tensed again. "Ya look tense, Kat!" Kyle observed.

"Go figure! We're talking about our womanly rights and…"

Kyle interrupted her fiery counter. "Womanly rights?"

"We're all having our weeks, Kyle," Liz turned in her seat and faced Kyle. Oh, Kyle thought, their weeks. He nodded.

"Lizzy!" Kat shouted and Marcus turned towards Kyle, resting his head on his other bent arm under his head.

"I'm up. Give me five more…" Marcus drawled.

"Shut up, Marcus." Kat replied.

"I don't think he heard you," Kyle stared at the rearview mirror. Valerie wasn't smiling now. She almost looked saddened and feared looking in the mirror at him again. Kyle studied the highway by the car. How the white lines spattered in the middle of the road. How some weren't even and they must have been done by someone who didn't care much. He looked again at the mirror but only saw half of Kat's frowning face. Valerie was leaned on Liz's shoulder and Liz's head on the top of Val's head. They must be getting a short nap before they came upon the site. Kyle checked his watch. 12:19 A.M. It wouldn't be long now. Kyle stared back at Kat in the mirror and got a look from her back. It was the cutting of a glance, but it was a look. Like he had killed Kat's favorite bird or some family pet.

"What'd I do, Kat?" Kyle finally asked.

"I told you we were discussing…"

"Cut the crap, Kat." Kyle cut her off again.

"Never mind," Kat said pulling a strand of too-short-to-braid hair behind her ear and put both of her palms on the top of the steering wheel.

"No. Don't never mind. Why the frown?" Kyle scooted up behind Kat again. He could feel her foot getting heavy as they talked and accelerated. He checked the speed-o-meter. It went up to eighty and then they started slowing again when Kat glanced at her digital green clock. She steadied them at seventy; possibly knowing her foot would get heavy again if he continued to talk. He still didn't get what he had said.

"About ten minutes and we'll be getting on another exit," Kyle said, knowing he was wrong.

"More like five," Kat pointed at a sign that told them of the Bull Head City/ Davis Dam exit road. "Then another eight, maybe."

"Unless you break the speed limit again."

"That road doesn't have a speed limit."

"That road is fifty-five according to state law."

"Didn't realize we read state laws," Kat said coolly.

"Have to know the laws to know if we're breaking them and when to look out for cops. If we know we are doing something wrong we can have an alibi. Those without alibis…"

"End up like Tony and Marcus, behind bars for a given amount of time by a distrustful man of the city."

"Aka judge?" Kyle asked hearing a lot of fear behind Kat's tone.

"Yeah." Kat took their exit and Liz and Val sat up for a second, slowly sat up, Kyle noticed. They knew they would bump heads if they sat up too quickly. They passed a small gas station, with those old two gas pumps out front. It looked to be closed but a vehicle sat out there. When they passed by the vehicle pulled out with no headlights. In the dark it looked to be black, maybe a coupe, possibly a Bentley. "We have a tail," Kyle said turning back around and looking Kat in the mirror.

"I see 'em." Kat said with the same coolness she kept since she didn't figure arguing with Kyle was a good idea.

"Just keep going to the site. If they turn on their headlights they'll probably end up passing us. If they ride up by us…"

"I'm slowing down. Thanks Kyle, Ian told me what to do in case of tails."

"Fine." Kyle hated being told off by a woman. It took a lot of manhood out of a guy. If they weren't in a car he could stare Kat down, he thought. Yeah, he could, he decided stubbornly. He glanced back at the car.

"Stop that," Kat said. "I can watch him in the mirror if you stop glancing back.

"Okay." Kyle shook Marcus awake.

"They're jerks I told you," he said sleepily.

"Man wake up and cut the crap. We ain't goin' to no school. Wake up!"

"I'm up, I'm up," Marcus slid up from his slouched position and looked at the girls lined up front and then at Kyle. "What's going on? Where are we?"

"Almost to Davis Dam; we're being tailed. Don't look back. Just know it's a dark colored coupe, maybe a Bentley. They've been following us, how long would you say Kat?" Kyle took his eyes off of Marcus' serious look and looked up at Katerina.

"Four going on five miles. We'll be to the site in three."

"Two, one," Marcus smirked.

"Ha, ha," Kat laughed dryly. Liz and Val snickered but hushed quickly. Marcus was just tired and in a tired state of mind got real loopy anyone could tell by the things he said in his sleep.

"We going to try to lose them or take them on with us?"

"I'm hoping they aren't a tail. They might just be some county boys wanting to play a game here. We passed a two-pump gas station back there where we picked them up."

"I hate kids." Marcus pronounced.

"No wonder he has a girlfriend," Liz laughed; Kyle decided pms brought out the giggles in girls. Val would be cracking jokes next.

Marcus grumbled. Kyle looked at him so he wouldn't say anything to Martin's girl. Last thing they needed was a trip in the wrong direction after getting back the other half of Marc's payment.

"Two miles," Kat replied speeding up.

"Don't speed up, Kat." Marcus yelled over the wind, grumpiness showing his demanding instructive side.

"I can speed up in my car if I want. If they are a tail, they'll speed up too, if they are just kids they wouldn't dare break the speed limit at this hour."

"Why, cause of the cops around?" Liz asked.

"Good question, Liz," Kyle looked from Liz to Kat and grinned.

"No, Liz." Kat smirked. "You know men can't drive as well as women at night.

"Crap," Marcus commented.

"*Mucho* crap," Kyle agreed.

Kat accelerated over sixty-five and Kyle was tempted to look behind him so he did. They were right on their tail, headlights on. "Great," Kyle said out loud. "Just great, Kat." She didn't slow until she came to the bridge over Lake Mead. A circle of vehicles was on the other side as Kat pulled up and cut her headlights. The tail coming around and parking next to Kevin's "truck" or a van that looked like it should be serving ice cream out of the side of it, except there was no window, as far as Kyle could tell.

Marcus hopped out of the backseat of the convertible and walked over to Tony to talk, Kyle decided. Tony had his arms crossed leaning against his Pontiac Firebird. May and Mandi were nowhere in sight. Kat, Liz, and Valerie walked over to Ian, and he laughed then smiled as Kyle walked around the front of the convertible looking at all the group. The two men from the car that had followed them, a blue coupe with a lightening streak down the driver's side, came into the circle of vehicle hoods. Kevin walked over to Ian as the men came up. Kat was frowning and Val and Liz seemed to be condoling her. They made a three-girl circle with hugs and condolences. Kyle leaned against the hood of the car and pulled out his pack of spearmint gum. Marcus joined him and Kyle offered a piece. Marcus took it reluctantly.

"I'd rather have a smoke," Marcus replied flicking the foil ball he had crushed toward the center of the circle.

"Thought Tony had them."

"Kat has some and Mandi has some. Mandi and May walked up to the bathroom at the museum about ten minutes ago, Tony said," Marcus explained nodding his head toward the coupe that had followed them in. "Tony said them guys are the deliverers. They have the coke." Marc glanced at where Kat had been standing with Liz and Val. "Looks like our girls are headed up towards the bathroom now. Guess they don't want to be around when we trade this junk."

"Ian probably Okayed it. Kat told him about our tail and he started laughing. I recognize those guys now. Those are two of May's friends, Ezekiel and Logan from the casino."

"No kidding?"

"Nope," Tony walked up by them and was flipping his cig toward Marcus.

"Thanks," Marcus breathed in and sighed the smoke out. "This is what I needed."

"Looked like it," Tony grinned at Kyle and walked over to where Ian, Logan, and Ezekiel stood. Ezekiel looked like he should be in drama movie or something. Kyle started to walk toward them and turned around quickly as Marcus chuckled. May was grinning behind him.

"Long time, no see, Stranger," said May, crossing her arms under her protruding white tee. Looked to be one of Tony's and it didn't quite fit May's broad shoulders. Kyle wasn't exactly looking at that though. She wore some black jeans too tight to be legal, Kyle thought.

"May, you demon. You don't even smell like pizza anymore. Windy ride?"

"Maybe. I freshened up just now too, though."

"For Logan or Ezekiel?"

"Hmm, does it show that much?" May looked over at Ezekiel and though Tony was over there Ezekiel looked back at May with lust in his eyes. It was dark out there except a dim street lamp off to the side near where Kat had parked. Kevin's truck made a shadow on the coupe. This was thought out thoroughly.

"Does what show?" Kyle started to ask.

Marcus interrupted him, "Their lust, Kyle. May's been screwing with Ez."

"Thanks for keeping me updated," Kyle snatched Marc's cig and handed it to May.

"Thanks," May sucked a bit on the end flirtatiously. Just getting a taste, she looked lovingly at Kyle then handed the cig to Kat who took it up naturally. May liked the danger of a cig. Tony smoked and maybe Ez smoked. May flipped her hair back over her shoulder as she walked up to Ez. They embraced in what would seem like old friends and then Ez's hand came down on May's rear and groped. Kyle shot his eyes at Tony, but he was in a conversation with Ian and Logan and hadn't noticed a thing of what his girl was going through. May giggled and the other girls surrounded behind her except Liz who had joined Martin over by Shawn's Grand Am and was making out for lost times, Kyle decided. He checked his watch wondering if one A.M. would come soon enough.

As he looked back at the larger circle of girls and Ezekiel, Kyle decided to walk over and overhear their discussion. On his way to walk over there, Shawn and Kevin met him on each side and strode him to the back of the van.

"How's it going, Man?"

"Not so good. You see what that punk is doing to Tony's girl?"

"May can handle herself," Kevin smiled pushing Kyle down on the back of his van where pizza boxes were now stacked.

"How long have ya'll been waiting?" Kyle asked looking around at the stacked and taped pizza boxes.

"Little over…" Kevin looked up at the stars.

"About twenty minutes give or take a minute," Shawn answered crossing his arms since he had let go of Kyle's arm.

"Tony knows about Ez huh?"

"No and he ain't gonna." Shawn said commanding Kyle in a fashion that could only be considered cool but truthful.

"I saw the shiner you gave my bro," Kyle said hoping to change the subject. He didn't care about their little May and Ezekiel secret if they didn't want him to.

"Yeah? You like that? Want one?" Shawn grinned.

Kevin laughed. He peeked around the side of his truck and then back at Kyle. "We don't want May getting in trouble because Tony found out something that's been going on for a couple of years."

"Yeah, Man. It's better to keep things under wraps ya know. Its not like Ian doesn't know. We just hate to lose Tony because of a girl he can't control, ya know?"

"I get ya," Kyle said standing up. "We leave at one? Right?" Kyle heard footsteps and hoped they were female.

"Ian wants to have a reunion before ya'll take off," Martin said, his arm around a giggling Liz's neck.

"We leave as soon as this reunion is over," Kevin shut the back of the truck and the three of them headed over to the circle with Kyle between Kevin in the lead and Shawn in the back of him. They didn't want him doing anything suspicious. He wouldn't now that he had been told.

Tony stood by Ian with crossed arms. Shawn joined him and pocketed his hooked thumbs on his leather pants. Martin and Liz were standing by Marcus and Kat. Marcus looked like he was keeping a fair enough distance from both. He looked at Kyle with a curious expression but Kyle only gave a shrug in return.

Kevin walked to the other side of Ian and talked with Logan some more before Ian interrupted the whispering and began his departure instructions. Kyle spotted Valerie just behind Ian. Ian had his arm around her waist and Kyle told himself it was a friendly gesture, not a loving one. Ian acted like a father sometimes since he was the oldest here. As far as Kyle knew he was the oldest between Logan and Ez too, but Kyle didn't care. He folded his arms and wished he could lean back on something, he crossed his ankles and chewed his gum looking around from Valerie to Kevin, Logan, Ez and May were holding hands and when Kyle looked for Tony, who wasn't far from him, they were just across the circle from Tony. Brave sons-of-bitches. Well, Bitch and son of... well... Kyle stopped thinking technicalities.

Randy stood beside Mandi in front of Martin's Grand Am, and Martin and Liz were there again, kissing and whispering smiley things in each other's ears.

"All right. I hope everyone has met Ezekiel and Logan Barr," Ian looked around the group as most of them nodded. Kyle looked at Tony. Was he boiling too or just sleepy, grumpy? Kyle decided not to push his luck with Shawn standing right there. Marcus mouthed to Kyle, 'Brothers?'

Kyle shrugged again. Why he didn't know. Brothers, cousins; who cared? Ez was laying his hands on Tony's girl.

"The truck leaves in seven minutes. Kyle and Kevin…"

"And Marcus," Kyle said loud enough to be heard by all.

"And Marcus," Ian continued, "will be goin' to the drop off site."

Kyle looked back at Shawn. His arms were crossed and his eyebrow furrowed, but besides that he looked relatively calm. Kyle knew this was a surprise idea all around, even to Marcus, who Kyle didn't look over to see his expression.

"I don't want to see any of you until tomorrow at one P.M." Ian was saying. "My pad will be having a pool party, I expect all of you to be there. Payment will be in a week; if you ain't at the pool party, you ain't on the list. You ain't on the list; you don't get paid. Any questions before we head out?"

"Tell them what happens if they get in jail before one, bro." Kyle looked over at Randy. His arm was around

Mandi; Mandi's arm was around Randy's waist and Randy was staring at Marcus the cutting his eyes back at Kyle.

"You go to jail," Ian replied looking around at his group. "You stay in jail for a week. That's a week without a lawyer. You get less than a week's sentence; think you'll be all right. Hmm? Any more questions?"

Kyle looked around at everyone. He noticed Valerie was walking around towards Tony's Pontiac Firebird. May kissed Ez's cheek and he started walking towards Logan. Everyone was breaking up, going into his or her own vehicles.

"Hold on a minute," Kyle waved Kevin towards the truck. He walked up to the middle of the circle where Marcus met him. They shook hands and hugged up.

"I can't believe you did that. I'm goin' to Mexico!"

"You better believe you are. Go wait with Kevin, I'll be there in a jiff," Kyle said letting go of Marcus' hand and stepped towards the Firebird where Val was leaning over to May's ear and they giggled as Kyle stopped near them. "Val."

"Kyle. Hey. You be safe. Hear?"

"I promise to be," Kyle smiled. He glanced back at the backseat of the Pontiac. Liz was saying goodbye to Martin it looked like. "You girls headed out together?"

May looked back at Kat's convertible. "Nah. Kat and Mandi are going to some club, meeting Randy and some of the boys there. I'm taking this squad out to celebrate and maybe go racing if Tony will give me the keys," she looked over at Tony, who was in a conversation with Logan and Ian again.

"Be right there, Babe," Tony called, turning his head for a second, the keys to his Firebird dangling from his forefinger.

"Wish I could see Mexico," Val said smiling, and blushing it looked like as she looked down at the road.

"Me too. Maybe some other time when it's not illegal stuff," Kyle stepped up in front of Val and took her waist in his hands. She was blushing. He bent his head down and pressed his lips to hers. Her arms seemed to automatically curl around his neck; she kissed him back.

"Man! Time's a running!" Shawn shouted.

"Looks like someone is hot enough over here, Ian!" May shouted. Tony tossed her his keys and grinned at her.

"I'll see ya at the track," Tony yelled.

"Thought you were riding with us!" May shouted back. "Traitor!"

"Naw, Babe. I just have wheels now," Tony hopped onto Randy's bike. Ian had done hopped on his bike and was headed slowly over the bridge, waiting on Tony to catch up.

Kyle looked back at Marcus and Shawn sharing some joke. He kissed Val's cheek and ran over to the truck. "You best get goin' too, Shawn."

Shawn pulled out a keypad, pushed a beeping noisy button, and unlocked his Grand Am. Shawn grinned.

"Hey Shawn you racing tonight?" May yelled.

"You better believe it Chica," Shawn replied passing behind Kyle. Great, Kyle thought. Shawn would be around his girl now.

"Man, get the girl off your mind and get your tail over here," Marcus yelled from the truck where he stood on the doorstep. Kevin was already behind the wheel, so Kyle ran to it. Marcus slid over into the middle and buckled up. Kyle got in and Kevin turned the key. "How many hours is this trip?" Marcus asked leaning his head back, turning it from side to side to look at Kevin then Kyle, to see who would answer.

"About four maybe five hours to Mexico. Then an hour of a plane ride." Kevin answered backing out, following the gang down the five-mile road that Kat had driven Kyle and Marcus out by; the road that the drug carriers had followed them on.

W hat's up?" Marcus yawned awake. Kyle had
fallen asleep too. He stretched his back and
looked over at Kevin as he stepped down out of the truck.
Kevin had pulled out at a rest stop.

"New driver and bathroom break," Kevin replied and
then he was gone.

"What's that sound?" Marcus asked. Kyle heard it
too: a beeping sound was coming from his back pocket.

"Oh," Kyle pulled out his cell. "Yeah?"

"Where you been man?"

"Asleep, Shawn? What's up?"

"Where did Val say she was going?" Shawn sounded serious. Kyle sat up feeling suddenly serious too.

"Why? She's not at the racetrack?" Kyle looked down at his watch. 2:30 A.M. "Maybe she's in bed."

"With who?"

"Hey now," Kyle said offended by Shawn's joke.

"No really, Man. She's from Chicago right?"

"Yeah…" Kyle wished Shawn would just come out with what he was saying about Valerie. So she was Chicago, what was he saying, that she was tough for the Vegas crowd?

"She doesn't know anyone that's not in the gang."

"Spill it out man, what's up?"

Another voice broke in. "Shawn? Shawn…"

"What's up?" Marcus shrugged as Kevin walked around from the driver's side back from the bathroom to Kyle's side.

All Kyle heard was muffled noises so he covered the mouthpiece and talked to Kevin. "Valerie is gone."

"Where?" Marcus asked.

"Shawn doesn't know." Kyle looked out the window. The borderline was heavily guarded. They could check the back; all they'd find was pizza boxes; they'd think it was really pizza right away.

"Where would she go? She's from Chicago," Kevin wondered out loud.

"That's what Shawn was saying."

"What's he saying now?" Kevin asked, looking content on standing just outside the passenger side door and worried.

"Nothing. It's like they are discussing something else. Shawn?" Kyle said into the mouthpiece taking his hand away.

"May, Mandi, Kat and Liz are gone. They were supposed to be in the bathroom."

"Maybe they are having a girl's night..." Kyle offered in stupor. He hoped that's all it was.

"They told us they were racing. They told you, remember. I'm going to call Ian, I'll call you with information when we get some." Shawn hung up after he had said that and Kyle told Marcus and Kevin what was going on as he got into the driver's seat and Kevin took the far passenger's seat.

"That's just weird. Do you really think it was a girls' night out surprise on us guys?" Marcus asked.

"No, but I'm hoping that's all it is. What else would it be?"

"Dude," Kevin said as Kyle pulled towards the borderline of the countries. "Women can be so freakish sometimes with their minds and … and their ways." Kevin leaned back looking out the window as Kyle showed the Mexican officials his passport and identification cards. He explained about the pizzas in the back for their lunch later and the officials didn't even ask to look in the back. They drove on by and Marcus looked over at Kyle, his head leaned back against the seat.

"Mexicans can be so fruity," Marcus commented.

"They aren't all like your *familia*," Kyle said remembering his Dad's reaction when he said he was going to America.

"Yeah, well where's this airport anyways?" Marcus changed the subject. Kevin was asleep all ready as they were only two miles past the borderline.

"Another ten minutes and we should be there." Kyle looked at his watch. "We're a little late. You think they are going to care?"

"Depends on how tired they are at 3 A.M. I guess."

"And how grouchy. But it's not quite that late yet." Kyle accelerated the truck up to fifty-five.

"Or that early," Kevin said his eyes closed. Kyle only thought he was asleep.

"Man, thought you were getting some shut-eye," Kyle replied.

"My eyes are shut, Genius."

"Ladies," Marcus said mocking Mandi's earlier comment. "We are all tired and possibly all grouchy; worried about our women."

"Your women," Kevin corrected.

"Our women," Marcus repeated. "I saw you with May earlier," Marcus patted Kevin's leg.

"Don't touch the jeans, Man," Kevin growled.

Marcus removed his hand and bent his elbow, laying his hand on his arm.

Kyle thought about how they left. Tony and Ian on bikes; Shawn in his Grand Am; Martin and Randy riding with Kat and Mandi? Where was Martin? Liz, Val, May and Martin? His cell rang again. He lowered his speed and pulled the phone out of his back pocket. "Yeah?"

"Where are you at?"

"Who…"

"It's Tony, where are you at?"

"Mexico; four miles south of the U.S. border. Approaching the airport."

"Goods are still in the back of your truck?"

"Yeah. Hey, you find the girls?"

"That's just it, Kyle. We think they are in Mexico."

"What? Why?"

"Why else?"

"They wouldn't do that. They…they…"

"Who's on the phone now?" Kevin raised his head and met Kyle's confused eyes.

"Tony," Kyle said shortly. "The girls might be in Mexico."

"No way," Marcus said sitting up from his relaxed position.

"Dude, this is getting so uncool," Kevin replied looking at the airport as they approached.

"What if they aren't here?" Kyle asked hopefully.

"Call me back let me know. If they do show, try to talk them out of it. I know you haven't been arrested or nothing man but Marcus might can talk them out of it. You can talk to Valerie at least. Tell her what happens if you get caught. They can't have the pizza boxes man."

"Understood, Tony. What are the rest of the guys doing while this is going on?"

"Calling the girls' families hoping we're wrong, waiting on word back from ya'll. I hope just as much as you do that they are out on a girls' night out freaking us out playfully. But if they want the boxes, please talk them out of this." Tony hung up. Kyle folded his phone and pocketed it again for the second time that night, worried as he did so.

May had to be leading the girls. They had been whispering and giggling all day. May wasn't the kind to giggle with girls. Kyle wondered for a minute if they were after the drugs, was Logan and Ezekiel behind it also?

"What's up now?" Marcus asked.

"Tony thinks the girls might be after the coke. For their own split, bigger cash or something. As soon as we get to the drop off site, we look around for them. If we don't see them by the time the coke is shipped out, we call Tony and confirm. If they are, Marcus, man, Tony wondered if you had any skills from getting arrested. Like talk May and them out of it all. This is really bad."

"Totally," Kevin agreed.

"I can probably handle that. Think they are loaded?" Marcus asked as Kyle sped back up down the highway towards the airport.

"Knowing Mandi," Kevin replied. "Yeah." He nodded nervously. "Why aren't we loaded?"

"Borderline man!" Marcus cut his eyes at Kevin. "You think them pizza boxes would look real if we brought guns?"

"We are so dead if they are out there. What are we supposed to do, go against Ian? No thank you."

"We'd have perks," Kyle heard Kevin say in a distant tone.

"Oh yeah, we could be their slaves. No thank you either," Marcus said. Kyle pulled up by the airport guard and gave him a card and a ticket pass to go around to hangar thirty to deliver pizzas. The guard let them through. Kyle drove around to the private jet hangar Ian had given him information on earlier.

"See any girls?" Kyle bent his head down looking around the air base.

"No, sadly," Marcus looked around smiling at Kyle.

"Keep your eyes opened." Kyle pulled by the hangar and looked around hoping the jet was inside the hangar still.

"You're late," Kyle heard a female voice say as he walked around to the back of the truck. "We were getting worried."

Kyle turned around and saw May, and then Liz, Mandi, Kat, and Valerie, arms around well-dressed Mexican men. May's hand was gripping a black leather bag. Her arms were male-free, but a Caucasian looking guy possibly American or Spanish-American had his arm around her waist. And it wasn't Ezekiel, Tony, or Logan. Kyle didn't recognize him. He frowned.

"You are supposed to be in the States," Kevin said walking around the truck.

"You were supposed to be here half an hour ago," Val retorted.

Kyle's fists balled by his sides. He spit out the flavorless gum. "You traded them for us!?"

"I traded your money for more money? Sure thing hot lips," Val replied.

"Calm down, big boy," said May, pulling out of the white guy's arms and dropped the bag in front of Kyle.

"What's that?" Kyle asked glancing from it to May's grin.

"Your payment. You don't tell Tony or Ian or anyone from the old clan you saw us. You get to split that between you and Kevin and Marcus if he's with you."

Marcus walked to the back of the truck and sat down on the bumper. "He is."

"Good."

"Not in on your deal, he's here, with his bro." Marcus explained. May frowned.

"Its more money than Ian offered you. And you get it all right now. What could be better than that?"

"He could take his arm off of my girl, for one," Kyle pointed at Val and the Mexican man she was wrapped up with.

"Since when is she your girl, Kylee?" Kat asked. May walked over to Kevin and slid her hand over his cheek. "What about you cherry-pie?"

"Who's the nerd?" Kevin nodded at the white guy standing alone now that May had walked away. May glanced back coolly, "Luke? He's not important except for this deal. We can end like that." May snapped her fingers. "What do you say Kevin? Ten thou a piece. No taxes, no bargains. You say yes and you're inside with us."

"What's the catch, May?" Marcus asked. May turned her attention to him, taking her hand off of Kevin's cheek.

"No catch," May batted her eyelashes and turned her body back towards her friends.

"How about the drugs?" Marcus questioned. Kyle looked on, hoping this was part of Marcus' good hold up plan.

"Luke's guys get the drugs," replied May as she linked her arm in Luke's arm and patted his forearm.

"This was more thought out than that wasn't it?" Marcus asked. Kyle pulled out a pack of gum. Val watched him. He betted each one of these girls hadn't had a smoke since they stepped into Mexican territory. Kyle folded the gum into his mouth and began chewing. He put the pack back in his back pocket, pushing a button that would record the rest of what they were saying. He pushed another button that cancelled all his further calls from the time the device started recording. Kyle crossed his arms on his chest as he chewed his spearmint and listened to Marc's stalling conversation.

"Maybe," answered Kat stepped forward, pulling her arm down from the middle Mexican's shoulder. "Maybe we got tired of being treated like mice."

"We needed something bigger, Kyle," Liz added.

"And we didn't need chickens," Val said after Liz.

"I loved you, Valerie," Kyle said. "Note loved. Now..." he waved his hand in the air. "I can't have you worth nothing. You know how Ian is."

"Better than you know," May replied.

"Way better," Mandi agreed.

"What's Randy going to do to you now?" Marcus asked Mandi.

"Who cares? Don't you get it, Marc, Ian was screwing us since he created this stupid clan. If we want to get screwed now, we choose our men."

"That's a lie," Kevin glanced at Kyle. "Ian wasn't screwing them. They'd get wasted on his crown royal and end up in his bed sure. Together, as a pack of girls. Ian told them they were getting it hard, and then he'd leave them there. Yeah, screwing ya'll, Mandi," Kevin looked back at the girls' faces. "He was screwing with ya'lls minds. Fooled ya good didn't he?"

Mandi seemed to be grinding her teeth. "Just open the truck, Marc."

"First you call Tony and tell him where you are," Kyle pulled his cell out and held it in front of May.

"Like hell! Open the truck, Kevin! Now," May pulled a .45 Colt from out of Luke's back pocket and held it in front of her.

"May you said no guns, Sweetie," Luke said.

"Ya'll shouldn't have brought them then," Kat yelled, pulling a gun in turn as the other girls pulled guns from the back of the other men's back pockets. Kat, Mandi, and Liz shot at Kyle and Marcus' feet. Kyle and Marcus ran around the front of the truck and ducked down. Kyle looked under the truck and could see feet. Them women were waltzing around a Mexican airport with loaded men and in heels no less! Kyle ran around the truck to see Kevin hauling the moneybag onto the plane; thirty grand gone. Kevin traded clans. For a woman's clan, Kyle thought, grimacing.

"I told you I was good," yelled May shooting at the van. "I just never told you how I got there! Watch the papers in Phoenix!" She shouted as Luke hauled her as one of the last passenger's into the jet.

Marcus yelled that the front of the van was on fire and if it reached the tank considering they hadn't filled it up recently since their fifth hour gas station stop it would blow the contents up. "Do you want to get the coke?"

"Not especially but we better!" Kyle yelled as the private jet flew off the runway and into the night. Kyle cursed himself and again when he cut into the pizza boxes and found nothing less than pizza. He heard it as Marcus grabbed him and pulled him onto the concrete runway. A sizzle and a whistle then a gas explosion was the van, the pizza, the papers and tickets and his friend, Kev was somewhere in a jet plane probably having Spanish cocktails.

"Dames," Marcus got up and walked towards the main airport where citizens boarded public planes; Kyle not far behind him. Their cuts from hitting the concrete and smudges of black from the fire's heat showed on their faces. He wiped perspiration off of his face and Marcus sat down on a wooden bench outside the entrance to the airport. Kyle pulled out his phone and called Ian's number. Tony answered, "Well?"

"We lost Kevin."

"Dead?"

"No, he went with the girls, the cash and possibly the drugs."

"Where's the truck?"

"In front of hangar thirty with fire and pizza chunks."

"Pizza chunks?"

"*Si.*"

"May, that double crossing..." Tony took a deep breath and voices changed as Kyle heard something rip or tear.

"Tony, stop it! What...What, Kyle?"

"May and the girls are in Mexico. Least I think they still are. They left on a private jet with an American looking guy named Luke and four Mexican men in sports jackets. They have a bag they said was thirty thousand dollars and..."

"A black leather bag?" Ian asked.

"Yeah. Wooden grip handle, looked new. They offered it to us told us it was cash."

"They were probably bluffing. Who did the most talking?"

"May," Kyle answered sitting down beside Marcus. Marcus' eyes were closed and his forehead was in his hands. He was sweaty and stunk just as bad as Kyle knew he did. The citizens looked at them disgustedly.

"I imagine it was the drugs we had not yet put in the pizza boxes."

"Shawn and Kevin said it was all packed up..."

"Where's Kevin now?"

"With them. Where's Shawn?"

"Not a clue," Ian said. "The rest of the boys are here at my pad awaiting news I'm going to hate to tell them. Are you two headed back tonight?"

"I doubt it. May blew up our van. I have a cell phone and my ID cards. My ticket back out of the borderline troops is burnt." Kyle explained hoping for Ian's assistance.

"Unfortunately I can't get you a ride out of there until after eight A.M."

"Fine." Kyle said relieved at anything he heard right now.

"But I can fly you directly out of the country and to the Vegas airport from there."

"That would be great," Kyle replied. "We got part of May's words and some of the other girls on my recording chip in my phone."

"Good job, Kyle. I'm sorry to say we won't be getting paid now. But I'm glad you stuck by us. Six down in one night... Well. No worries about it right now. How is Marcus, he hold up?"

"He talked the best he could. He's halfway to dreamland now."

"Good. Ya'll get some rest. I'll see you personally at 8 A.M., hangar five, will that be okay?"

"Great, thanks Ian."

"Good. Talk to you then."

"Bye," Kyle hung up and put his phone in his back pocket with his ID cards and gum pack. "Hanger five at eight A.M. Marc. We'll be in Vegas by ten tomorrow morning." Kyle looked at his watch, it read 3:19 A.M.

"What time is it now?" Marcus drawled his question out, probably aching as much as Kyle was.

"Three twenty."

"I hate waiting," Marcus said. Kyle smiled. They'd find another job by next month... without dames.

A month later.

We on for Chicago?"

"Hold on," Tony walked into the room interrupting Ian, Marc, and Kyle's finishing touches on their next job.

"What?" Ian asked, as Tony hit the kitchen counter in Ian's pad with a Phoenix newspaper. That's all Kyle caught as the paper was turned upside down, so that Ian could see it right side up. "What you got here, Tony?"

"Guess where May and the girls are right now?"

Kyle looked down at the paper. "Guadalupe bank roll stolen. Six U.S. citizens arrested carrying ten pounds of cocaine..." Kyle stopped reading to himself. He looked up at the grin on Tony's face. "They're in jail?"

"Mexican jail. Ten to fifteen years."

"And that makes you happy?" Marc asked.

"Oh yeah. That girl has been cheating on me for so long it was just about time she got hers."

"Ha! You knew about her and Ezekiel?" Kyle asked.

"Yeah; her and Logan; her and Kevin; her and Ian..." Tony looked up at the smile disappearing into a offended frown on Ian's face.

"I didn't do nothing but sleep with her man. I don't care if you believe me or not."

"Kevin could side with you," Marcus said. "He explained that much to us before he took off."

"Yeah, I remember something about that from the tape Kyle let us hear," Tony replied.

"Yep," Kyle nodded. "We're not giving them an attorney are we?" Kyle looked at Ian.

"Nope. Everyone ready to go to Chicago?" Ian clapped his hands together and rubbed them greedily.

"Where's the other guys?"

"Kyle, we went over this, earlier this morning. Martin's getting the plane tickets; Randy's got our luggage we packed last night," Marcus explained numbering people by holding out his hand. "Ezekiel and Logan are flying from Reno to meet us at Chicago; and we are meeting Randy and Martin in the terminal in," Marcus looked at his new watch. Though they had lost the job money, Ian had given each guy a one hundred dollar bill bonus for sticking with the gang. Marcus got him a digital watch like Kyle's but newer and as many cig packs as he could buy with the remainder of his pay. "Twenty minutes, if we get on the road right now."

"If we speed we can get there in fifteen minutes."

"No speeding in my coupe."

"Let's take my Firebird then."

"Notta chance," Kyle said grinning.

"There's this chick at the airport…" Tony grinned walking out to the coupe in front of Kyle, Marcus, and Ian.

"NO DAMES ON THE JOB!" Kyle shouted simultaneously with Ian and Marc. The new rule in the gang was bliss. No temptations equaled a finished job and money for all.

The End.

Printed in the United States
by Baker & Taylor Publisher Services